For Ben, the deep-sea diver and protector of the ocean

www.dragonbloodpirates.co.uk

ORCHARD BOOKS
338 Euston Road, London NW1 3BH

First published in 2008 by Lothian Children's Books,
an imprint of Hachette Livre Australia
First published in the UK in 2011 by Orchard Books

ISBN 978 1 40830 825 7

A CIP catalogue record for this book is available from the British Library.

10 9 8 7 6 5 4 3 2 1

Printed in Great Britain by CPI Bookmarque, Croydon

Orchard Books is a division of Hachette Children's Books,
an Hachette UK company.

www.hachette.co.uk

The Sorcerer's Death Mask

Dan Jerris

ORCHARD BOOKS

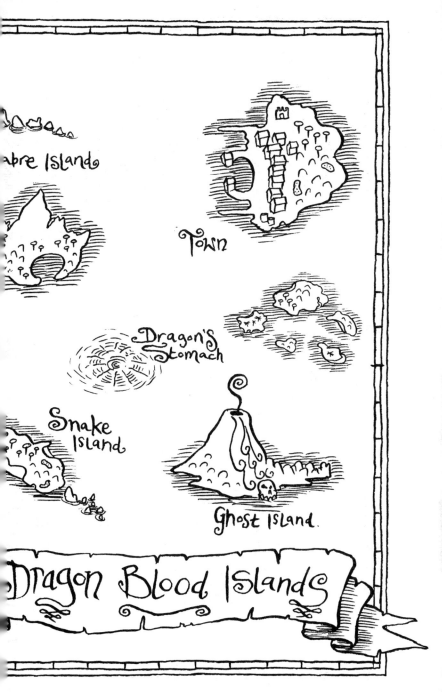

abre Island

Town

Dragon's
Stomach

Snake
Island

Ghost Island.

Dragon Blood Islands

Pirate Mateys
and Scallywags

Alleric (Al) Breas: Lives in Drake Drive and owns a mysterious sea trunk that takes him to the Dragon Blood Islands

Blacktooth McGee: A very nasty pirate who runs the brigantine *The Revenge*

Demon Dan: An evil pirate who died on Dragon Island and whose black diamond became stuck between a dragon's teeth

Evil Pearl: A deathless pirate who becomes Queen of Pearl Island and sacrifices people to a sea monster

Flash Johnny: Blacktooth's devious and greedy cabin boy

Grandfather: Mahoot's grandfather and guardian of the swimming elephants on Sabre Island

Greeny Joe: A shark so big and old that mould grows on his skin, making him glow green in the dark

Grenda: Snotty Nell's daughter

Gunner: The pirate captain of the ship *The Invincible*

Halimeda (Hally) Breas: Al's younger sister

Mahoot: Captain Gunner's cabin boy

Mozzy: *The Invincible*'s bosun – small and fast

Joe Seabrook: Al's best friend

Pigface McNurt: Blacktooth's bosun; a huge pirate with a ring through his nose

Prince Alleric: The prince who once ruled Sabre Island but disappeared in mysterious circumstances

Princess Haree: The princess of Ruby Island

Razor Toe: A deathless pirate who has enslaved the people of Ruby Island

Sharkbait: Snotty Nell's one-legged bosun

Slicer: *The Invincible*'s cook

Snakeboot: A magical white three-legged cat with purple eyes. Legend has it he once belonged to a terrifying pirate called Vicious Victor.

Snotty Nell: A horrible one-eyed pirate who sails a worn-out Indiaman called *Nausi VIII*

Stanley Spong: A crooked, sneaky trader in town who cheats people

Vampire Zu: Snotty Nell's huge first mate

Velvetfoot: A fearsome pirate distinctive for his velvet shoes that let him creep up on his victims unannounced

Vicious Victor: A pirate ghost. He used to pillage the Dragon Blood Islands and stole the magical sabre and scabbard that belonged to Prince Alleric.

The Missing Diamonds

Al Breas and his best friend Jack Seabrook were sailing through the Dragon Blood Islands on *The Invincible*, with Captain Gunner at the helm. Al peered through the morning mists as Sabre Island came into view. His heart raced at the idea of exploring Alleric Castle once again. There were so many secrets in the ruins.

"We're gunner drop anchor by

mid-morning," said Captain Gunner. He glanced down at Al's waist. "Though I must say I'm a bit worried about where you hid your sabre and scabbard. You don't want someone nasty stealing them."

"They won't," said Al confidently. "They're somewhere very safe."

"Nothing's safe around here," said Gunner. "It might be better if you gave them to me. Perhaps you should tell me where they are."

Al shook his head. "Sorry, Gunner, but I can't tell you. I don't think the scabbard's safe to wear, which is why I've hidden it. Even though we've found one of the missing black diamonds, we have to find all four before the scabbard will work properly and make its wearer invincible. One black diamond on its own is a terrible thing. It makes its owner deathless."

Years earlier, an evil pirate named Vicious Victor had stolen the Scabbard of

Invincibility from its owner, Prince Alleric, and, not realising the immense powers of its black dragon diamonds, had ripped them from the scabbard and given them to four of his pirate friends. Al and Jack had since found the scabbard, as well as the Dragon Blood Sabre, but were now trying to restore their powers by locating the missing black diamonds.

Gunner shrugged, disappointed at Al's answer. "Well, you can trust me," he said. "I'm not gunner get nasty, but I wouldn't mind being deathless. Are you sure you won't tell me?"

Al was tempted to laugh. The sabre and scabbard were hidden in Al's house: in number five Drake Drive, back in the twenty-first century. Gunner would never understand that Al and Jack had arrived in the Dragon Blood Islands by stepping into a magical sea trunk that had once belonged to

Al's grandfather and which now sat in
Al's attic.

Al's thoughts were interrupted by
the arrival of his friend Mahoot, who
clambered up on deck, carrying a
three-legged white cat.

"Snakeboot's getting lazy," said Mahoot.

"He was just sitting on the cushion in the cabin, purring. He needs some action."

"Like helping us find more treasure?" said Captain Gunner hopefully.

The Sorcerer of Dragon Island

The following day everyone on *The Invincible* searched Alleric Castle for signs of hidden treasure. As the hours wore on, Gunner and his crew gave up and returned to the ship. The boys were not so easily discouraged and continued exploring, following Snakeboot as he wandered from room to room.

Eventually, Snakeboot went into an empty hallway and sat by a window.

"I give up," said Mahoot, looking around. "There's nothing here."

"Come on, Snakeboot," Jack urged. "Show us something."

Snakeboot purred. "If Snakeboot's sitting down, it could be a clue," said Al. "We should look at the wall paintings again, like we did last time we were here."

"And look for another keyhole where my elephant ring might fit," said Mahoot. "We know Prince Alleric used my ring as a key to secret cupboards and things."

"Good idea," said Jack. "Last time it was in an elephant painting. Let's look at the elephants painted on the walls."

"I wonder what *my* ring is for," said Al, looking at the ruby-eyed dragon ring he wore on his thumb. "Maybe it's a key, too."

It didn't take the boys long to find a painted elephant with three tiny holes in its body. Excitedly, Mahoot pressed his elephant ring into each of the holes in turn. It worked! Soon there was a loud click and the slow grinding of wheels, then the wall swung inwards, revealing a secret study, filled with books.

On a table, covered in years' worth of dust, a book lay open as if it had been left half-read.

"This might be worth a look," said Al. He sat at the table and turned to the book's cover. It was called *The History of the Sabre.* "Check this out," he said. "There's heaps in here about the making of the Dragon Blood Sabre and the Scabbard of Invincibility."

Mahoot and Jack peered over Al's shoulder as he turned the brittle pages. "According to this, the prince of Alleric Castle back then had the sabre and its scabbard forged by a magician who lived on an island of dragons." Al pointed to a drawing of the magician in the book. "This sorcerer first made the sabre and gave the prince some magical words so it would take him through space and time." Al turned a few more pages before he continued the story. "But when the sorcerer made the scabbard he took four scales from a dragon and, with a magical forge, created four black diamonds. Then further on it says, '... The great prince paid a king's fortune for his magical weapon and, pleased with his treasures, he decided to order more wonders from the sorcerer on Dragon Island. He returned a year later to collect two magical rings: a dragon with ruby eyes for his son, and a pearl one for his daughter...'"

"They must be the rings Vicious Victor gave you and your sister," said Mahoot. "Isn't that strange?"

"It sure is," said Al, looking at his ring with new interest.

"Read on," urged Jack.

Al turned back to the pages. "'...While the prince was on the island, the sorcerer died. Amidst much wailing and grief, his body was buried in a golden coffin, clothed in silver, and a golden death mask set upon his face. His powers while he was alive were so immense that everyone feared him even in death, and no one dared touch his vast treasure. They buried everything with him and shut the door to his crypt.

"'Once the sorcerer was sealed into his tomb, the dragons on the island suddenly began to attack. The people, fearing they'd be hurt, and believing the island to be an evil place haunted by his ghost, left Dragon Island never to return. No one goes there now and...'"

Al read on silently, then said, "It seems the prince knew how to get back to the island, and it says here that he followed a map and returned there." He flipped through the remaining pages. "But there's no map in this book."

"Well, I reckon the story's a clue, at least, to finding the treasure," said Jack. "That'll make Captain Gunner happy."

"A golden death mask," said Mahoot, reflecting on the story. His eyes lit up with adventure. "I'd love to see a mummy in a tomb covered in gold."

"What's this?" said Jack, pulling at a

bookmark he'd just noticed, sticking out from the last page. "There's something written on it: 'What moves on four legs, then two legs, then three legs?'"

"That's easy enough," said Al. "A person. A baby crawls, a man walks, and an old man uses a walking stick. But why would anyone leave this in the book?"

"Maybe it's a clue to the Dragon Island Treasure?" said Jack.

"But what about these numbers?" asked Mahoot.

Al looked at the bookmark. Next to the question, someone had written '7D, 120L, 42'. Al thought for a while, then replied, "We're in a study full of shelves and books. The code must relate to them somehow ... Maybe what we need to do is find a book about man, or the ages of man, or the history of man and the letters and numbers will tell us where to find it. 7D could mean we should look seven shelves down; 120L might mean count 120 books to the left; and 42 could tell us the page number."

The boys counted quickly and discovered a large volume called *The Human History*. Within minutes they were holding a map of Dragon Island.

Demon Dan and the Dragon Diamond

Many years before Al and Jack had come to the Dragon Blood Islands, an evil pirate, Demon Dan, crewed for Vicious Victor on his ship. Dan's cruelty and greed were second to none, so Victor promoted him, giving him a ship and a rare black diamond as thanks for his years of loyal service.

The black diamond's glittering fire fascinated Dan so he took to wearing it as an earring. It was then he began to dream of becoming the richest man in the world.

As time went on, many a treasure ship fell to Dan's demonic attacks and, with each passing year, he became greedier and nastier until even his own crew hated him. "He's the worst pirate captain ever," complained Dan's first mate. "And he never gives us our dues."

As the treasure in the ship's hold grew heavier, the first mate roused the pirate crew into a murderous mutiny.

And so, one morning, when Demon Dan came on deck, he found his ruthless cut-throats waving their weapons. "Capt'n Dan!" called the first mate. "Stand down or we'll have your guts for garters!"

"We're fed up!" cried another brigand. "You haven't shared the plunder!"

"Scurvy dogs!" Captain Dan shouted. "Go

back to your duties or I'll make you walk
the plank."

"All of us? Impossible!" said a heavily
scarred man.

"Pirate law demands you treat us fair!"
shouted another.

"Pirate law!" yelled their captain. "You're
on my boat and they're my laws. No man's
taking my treasure."

One of the crew levelled his musket.
"Fine. You've given us no alternative:
we're taking over the ship!" he bellowed.
The gun boomed, the shot wounding Dan
in the chest.

The demon pirate shook himself, stepped
forward and smiled, his black diamond
earring glinting evilly. He pulled his sword
and leapt among his mutinous crew, slashing
at them in fury.

Some pirates grabbed muskets as their
captain attacked single-handedly, while others

fell upon Dan, brutally stabbing him with knives and swords. But the captain barely flinched from their blows and ruthlessly cut down all who stood against him.

When Dan finally cornered the last terrified members of his crew, they threw down their weapons and begged mercy from their deathless captain. Their reward was to

walk the plank at the end of his sword.

With all his crew dead, Dan sailed onwards until he anchored at a remote island teeming with dragon-lizards.

Exploring ashore, Dan came across an abandoned city and an immense castle, beneath which was a burial crypt, almost hidden, filled with jewels and treasures heaped around a golden sarcophagus. Inside the coffin was a mummified body, cloaked in silver robes and a death mask of solid gold.

In this dark place, away from the eyes of men, Dan rested for several days before unloading his treasure ship and making the island his home.

But Dan, rich beyond belief, became terrified that others would come to the island and steal his riches. He set traps to protect his fortune and vowed that no man would ever leave the island alive. "This will be my kingdom," he had sworn to himself. "I'll stay here forever as King of Dragon Island."

Years went by, and anyone who had the misfortune to set foot on Dragon Island was hunted down and fed to the dragons. In this way the island remained secret, and Dan, besotted by his jewels, believed himself indestructible.

However, one fateful day a hungry dragon sneaked up on Dan. It leapt forward, lunging with its razor-sharp teeth. With one bite it tore the black diamond from the pirate's ear.

With a bloodcurdling cry, Dan fell to the ground and his bullet-ridden heart stopped beating. The dragon tore him to pieces, but Dan's ancient flesh was too putrid to swallow, so the dragon left his body alone. Even the worms avoided the evil corpse, so it simply lay, rotting where it fell.

The black diamond, however, remained lodged between the dragon's front teeth. The dragon grew older, bigger and nastier, and made the entrance to the crypt its home.

The Map of Blood

Snotty Nell was sitting on the beach on Snake Island, waiting for her crew to bring back some rare and delicious orchid roots, which would be made into her favourite drink, sahlep. It was a drink that calmed her nerves and helped clear her mind. She wanted to think of a way to avenge herself on Captain Gunner, who had recently beaten her to a bountiful treasure and forced her to

sail a worn-out old Indiaman, the *Nausi VIII*.
"I need to get rich quick so I can get a better
boat and sink him," she muttered to herself.

Snotty's daughter, Grenda, was in the
dunes nearby, singing a little song while
trying to remember some strange dance steps
that Jack had once taught her. As she tried
to do the 'moon walk', she stumbled over
a skeletal hand. Curious, she dug around
the bones with her hands until something
glittered between her fingers. "Mum!" she
called. "A diamond!"

The word diamond electrified Snotty.
She raced to her daughter's side and, within
minutes, a corpse lay facing up at the sun,
clutching a bark-wrapped parcel to its ribs.
Snotty ripped the bark away, uncovering an
old shirt containing several more diamonds
within its folds. She was about to toss the
shirt away when the strange design on the
fabric attracted her attention. She looked

closer, realising she was looking at a letter,
written in blood. She spread the shirt flat on
the sand and began to read aloud.

"'…*Whoever finds my po'r body, hear
my tale. Our ship found'd upon a strange
island. We went ashore for rep'r. Dragons
beset us, eat'n some alive. The rest of us
ran, scatter'n in fear. One of my mates
met with a hermit, who attack'd 'nd cut
my mate to ribbons. Minutes later an'ther
of my crew arriv'd 'nd fought the hermit.*

My shipmate skewered him good with his cutlass. But the dreadful fiend still liv'd. My friend ran in terr'r. The deathless creature hunt'd him down, runn'n him through.

"'Afraid 'nd alone, I went to my boat, but I was beat there. My boat was afire. I follow'd the murderous hermit and found his hidey-hole. One day, while he were away, I crept inside, dodg'n booby traps, and discover'd a crypt. My eyes could not believe the jewels and treasure hidd'n there, or his demonic golden coffin. In fear that hell'd devour me if I stay'd, I grabb'd a few jew'ls, ran for my life, and cast myself into the sea, begg'n mercy of the ocean.

"'Tides 'nd currents brought me here, but with each pass'n day I know my end is nigh. For the finder of my body, I have drawn a map with my own blood. Take my jew'ls, revenge me and destroy the evil hermit who kill'd my friends.'"

Snotty turned the shirt over and, to her delight, found a map. "Treasure!" she cried. She wiped her dripping nose, rolled on her back and laughed.

As the *Nausi VIII* wallowed through the ocean, Snotty Nell sat upon the poop deck enjoying her sahlep tea. "No old deathless hermit ghost and no dragon will stop me from getting treasure," she promised herself. "This treasure's all mine because no one else knows anything about it." As she sipped on her drink, the scent of cloves, cinnamon, honey and something rare and fragrant drifted from her large tin mug and floated into the air.

But behind *Nausi VIII* another creature

followed the scent, which reminded it of the most delicious morsel of flesh it had ever tasted. As it followed Snotty's ship, its green dorsal fin cut the water.

Attacked by Dragons

The exploration party from *The Invincible* laboured up a steep hill on Dragon Island. Gunner led the way, following the map. Al stopped to wipe sweat from his brow.

"Can't see any dragons," puffed Jack, coming up beside him.

"I need a rest," said Mahoot. "It's just so hot."

"Gunner!" yelled Al. "We'll catch up with

you in a minute!" Gunner turned and waved and his men clambered onwards, up and over the hill.

"We should've thought to bring water," grumbled Mahoot.

A skitter of stones made the boys turn, and a lizard, about a metre long, came towards them. Its black tongue tasted the air as it eyed them suspiciously.

"It looks like a little komodo dragon," said Al.

"It's small," said Mahoot, sounding disappointed. "I was hoping to see a real dragon."

"What's that then?" gasped Jack, paling rapidly and pointing towards a shadow.

From the shade, an enormous lizard slithered into the sunlight. It hissed, snapped its long teeth and charged towards them.

"Run!" shouted Al, and the boys took to their heels.

As they raced up the hill, they almost collided with Gunner's crew hurtling back down. "Get to *The Invincible* fast!" Gunner bellowed. Thundering behind the crew were several enormous fast-moving reptiles.

Suddenly, everywhere, dragons crawled from the rocks. Forced to a halt, the crew bunched together while the hissing creatures circled. Finally one of the dragons darted forward, its jaws dripping with saliva.

"What'll we do?" cried Mozzy, the bosun.

"Kill it," replied Gunner, firing his musket. The shot glanced off the monster's hide.

"Now what?" asked Slicer, the cook, as the dragon hissed angrily and closed in.

"Aim at its eyes!" Al shouted.

In response, several shots split the air. The dragon shook its fractured head and crashed to the ground. Attracted by the smell of blood, the other dragons leapt upon it.

During the dragons' feeding frenzy Gunner and his men took their chance to back away to a safe distance and, feeling braver, pushed on towards the sorcerer's city.

Golden turrets, empty houses and paved streets echoed to their footsteps. Gunner's men, mouths open in awe, dared not speak in the gloom of the eerie, abandoned city.

"It seems the story was true," whispered Mahoot. "This place is spooky."

"It's amazing," breathed Jack, as he took in the magical symbols on the high turreted walls of a large building. "Do you think this is the sorcerer's castle?" As he gazed upwards, Jack tripped over something.

"Yuck, there's a man's leg just lying here!"

"It's odd the dragons haven't eaten it," said Al, puzzled.

"And there's a pair of arms," said Mahoot, pointing. "And a body over there, beside that wall." Everyone tiptoed carefully over to it, watching for danger. The dead man lay face up, his lips twisted in an evil sneer. His mottled skin was punctured with scars and wounds that had never healed.

"He's dead, but not rotted," Mahoot observed.

"It's like he's still alive," agreed Al, shaken by the man's pale eyes staring angrily at the sky.

"He reminds me of Razor Toe, the deathless pirate," said Jack. "He has the same horrible skin."

"It's like he's deathless, but he's dead," said Al. "Something weird's happened to him. I wonder what it is..."

"Whatever it is," said Gunner, "I'm not gunner stay in this spooky place longer than we have to. Let's find the burial place of that sorcerer."

They trudged on until they rounded a corner, entering the castle courtyard. Their arrival disturbed a massive dragon living in the crypt tunnel. It sniffed the air and, sensing dinner, uncurled. Seeing men, it bolted from the tomb, jaws snapping.

The startled pirates fired their muskets wildly at the beast. Some of the bullets hit their mark, splattering the flesh on the monster's head. But the mighty creature only paused, shook its head, opened its jaws and roared. As it did, the sun flashed against a dark diamond stuck between its razor-sharp teeth.

"Look!" said Jack, pointing at the diamond. "That explains a few things." Before he had time to say more, the terrible lizard recovered and charged.

Al looked wildly around and, spying a small doorway off to their left, shouted, "Over there!"

Everyone bolted to the doorway and squeezed inside as the lizard skidded to a halt outside.

"Now what?" asked Gunner, as the dragon rammed itself against the doorway, shaking the walls. "We're stuck in some sort of storeroom with no escape. Do we die in here, or go out there and fight like men?"

"Perhaps it'll get sick of waiting," suggested Jack. "Then we could sneak off back to the boat."

"I'm not gunner leave without treasure," said Gunner. "Perhaps there's a way to distract it."

As the sun set, the deathless dragon rested with its mangled head on its razor claws, never blinking, waiting and watching for the men to make their move.

The following morning, Snotty Nell, Grenda and the crew from the *Nausi VIII* found their way into the sorcerer's city after battling several small lizards. "I hate this place," Snotty grumbled, wiping dragon blood from her sword.

"Argh, but the gold'll be worth it," Vampire Zu, her first mate, reminded her. "According to your map, the tomb is close by."

Snotty smiled at the thought of a crypt full of treasure. "We're going to be very rich indeed," she chortled, as they rounded a corner. But to her shock, a mighty reptile blocked their way.

Their arrival had caught the dragon's eye. It had moved its head from side to side while its slow brain tried to work out who it should eat first – the men who were trapped in the storeroom, or the ones on the other side of the courtyard? Slowly, the dragon

stood and took a couple of steps towards
Snotty's crew.

Gunner peeped out of the room and gave
a cry. "Snotty! Help! We're trapped!"

Snotty went rigid at the sound of
Gunner's voice. "Is that you, Gunner?" she
shrieked.

"Yes, save us!" Gunner pleaded. "We need help!"

"Help you, you snivelling coward?" yelled Snotty, furious at being beaten to treasure once again. "We've killed at least ten lizards, and you're hiding, afraid of one. I hope it has you for dinner!"

"You can't kill it!" cried Gunner. "It's magical. We need help."

"As if anyone would believe that!" Snotty shouted. She turned to her crew. "Let's leave," she told them. "We'll find another way to the crypt before that stupid lizard comes after us." She led her men away from the courtyard, leaving Gunner to his fate.

But as Snotty left, the sea breeze blew up from the ocean, carrying her scent with it.

The dragon had just decided to sit down and wait for its dinner to come out of the storeroom, when it smelled something delicious. It lifted its giant head and sniffed the air. It was rare and mouth-watering. It was something the dragon had never tasted before, something worth hunting down. The animal stood, turned, and lumbered out of the courtyard. With its giant tongue flickering, tasting the air, it began tracking its fragrant prey.

The Crypt

Freed from the dragon, Gunner's crew made their way into the crypt's tunnel. "What's that stench?" asked Gunner, sniffing the heavy air.

"Lizard poo," Jack grumbled, stepping on something sticky.

Mahoot almost stumbled over a pile of torches. "We'll need these," he said, holding one out to Mozzy. Soon a spark flared, a torch flamed and a brightly decorated corridor leapt into life.

"Ah, look! The ceiling's painted with

beautiful birds," said Al, pointing upwards. As he did so, he noticed that the ruby eyes on his dragon-head ring were glowing. The further he moved towards the crypt the brighter the ring became, until even Gunner noticed the shining rubies.

"What's with your ring?" he asked. "It's like the stones are alive."

Distracted by the glowing rubies, Al didn't watch his step. Suddenly there was a sharp jerk on his ankle. He was pulled fiercely off his feet, whisked upwards and slammed against the ceiling. He came to his senses in the flickering torch light, hanging head down.

"Al, don't panic. You've been caught by a snare," Jack told him as Al began struggling.

"Stand fast, mateys!" ordered Gunner, pulling his sword. He sliced through the rope and Al fell to the floor with a thud. Catching his breath, he dusted himself down, noticing that the ruby eyes on his ring were dull once again.

"Keep your eyes peeled," Gunner warned. "Take each step with care."

Al moved forward shakily, and a few moments later they came to a heavy door. The ruby eyes glimmered back into life. "They're a bit like traffic lights," said Jack, noticing the glow. "On, off, on."

"You're right," agreed Al. "They are like traffic lights. But stop for what?"

As Gunner began to push at the door, the ring continued to grow brighter until Al sensed the danger. "Gunner! Stop!" he cried. "I think this door is booby-trapped!"

Gunner stepped back. "Everyone get down," he warned as he carefully ran his fingertips around the doorway. Soon he found a wire attached to the door. He freed it and gently pushed the door inwards.

Inside they discovered a rack of arrows,

drawn tight on a massive bow, ready to fire at point-blank range. Gunner clapped Al heartily on the back. "We'd be carrion meat if you hadn't warned us," he said.

Then all eyes moved past the deadly arrows as their torches lit a gigantic tomb, filled with statues of ivory, jars of fragrant oils, rolls of silk, woven carpets, crystal jars, alabaster plates and piles of gold and silver. In the middle of the room was a golden sarcophagus.

While Gunner's pirates raided the tomb, the boys went to the coffin. With caution, they lifted the golden lid. Inside was a body wrapped in silver brocade, wearing a golden death mask, inlaid with precious stones.

"This is like finding a pharaoh's tomb," said Al, "but it is a sorcerer lying here. I wonder if the mask is magical, like my ring, and the sabre and the scabbard?"

"The mask is so beautiful it should be in

a museum," said Jack, "but I don't think we should touch it, in case something weird happens."

"It's worth a king's ransom," said Gunner, coming up behind them. "If I had that mask, I could sell it for a fleet of boats." He reached out greedily to pull the cover from the corpse's face.

Al's ruby-eyed ring burned brightly again. "Watch out," he warned. "I think there's danger."

"There's no danger that's gunner stop me from taking this," said Gunner, his hands hovering greedily over the mask.

"I wouldn't if I were you," said Al firmly. "I've read about things in tombs that are cursed. What if it's covered in poison? My ring's telling you not to take it. There's loads of other treasure. Really, Gunner, leave it alone."

Gunner reluctantly straightened. His hands dropped to his sides. "Well, you've been right before," he said, turning away from the coffin. "Men," he called, "take as much as you can. We're gunner fill the holds of *The Invincible* to the brim!"

The pirates cheered and the lights in the ruby eyes of Al's ring faded.

Lizard Lunch

On the way back to the ship Al thought about the black diamond he'd seen sparkling in the hideous dragon's mouth. He turned to Jack. "I don't think that big lizard's going to give us that diamond," he said.

"And I have no idea how we could get it from him," said Jack.

"Speaking of that," interrupted Mahoot, "look over there." He pointed down the hill to where Snotty was running for her life, dodging between rocks, as the dreadful lizard charged after her.

"And there's the rest of her crew," said Jack, pointing further off. "It looks like they're surrounded by lizards and they're not having much fun."

"At least it means Snotty's pirates have taken them away from us," said Gunner, stopping to watch the drama. "It gives us more time to collect the treasure." He signalled to his men. "Come on," he ordered. "Hurry! Back to the ship."

The boys were about to follow Gunner, when Mahoot pointed towards a large boulder down the hill and off to the left.

Just below them, Grenda was in trouble. She was on one side of a rock, while a middle-sized dragon was on the other. As she turned to run, the dragon moved to face her, before twisting, blocking her path and any chance of escape.

"If it wasn't so awful I'd laugh," said Jack. "Perhaps we should try to help her.

The dragon's not that big."

"It's big enough to take a chunk out of her...and us," said Mahoot.

"She's always helped us," said Al. "We could do something: Jack, you've got a sword, and Mahoot, you've got a knife. It'll only take a minute to frighten off something that small, and Gunner won't miss us for a bit."

The boys clambered downhill towards Grenda, who was trembling in fear. As they got close to the lizard, they drew their weapons and charged, shouting loudly. The creature, startled by the sudden noise, turned tail and scuttled off.

Grenda slumped to the ground, exhausted, but when she recovered she looked up at the boys with pleading eyes. "Mum's in trouble," she sobbed, and a tear trickled down her cheek. "That humungous dragon is chasing her, and Gunner was right: we can't kill it. Vampire Zu stabbed it and it just flicked him out of the way with its tail, it was so keen to eat Mum! It didn't even stop to eat Sharkbait when he tripped and fell down in front of it!" Beginning to sob uncontrollably, she wailed, "I don't want my mum to die!"

"That dragon's a bit like Greeny Joe," said Jack, referring to the predatory shark. "It's following your mum everywhere." He patted Grenda's shoulder sympathetically. "But there's nothing we can do to save her. That lizard's indestructible and your mum seems to have caught its eye."

"Or its nose," said Al. "I reckon she must smell different from other people or something. Isn't she the only one on your boat who drinks sahlep?"

"Yes, she loves it," said Grenda, trying to sniff back her tears. "Sahlep's valuable and rare. Mum'd kill anyone who took some. And yes, you're right, Greeny Joe is always trying to eat her, ever since biting her face. That shark's even followed us here to Dragon Island!"

"So both the dragon and Greeny Joe love your mum," said Al. He thought for a moment and his face became serious. "Grenda, I have an idea. Do you have any sahlep on your boat?"

"A few bags," replied Grenda.

"And do you have any meat?" asked Al.

Grenda nodded. "What have you got in mind?" she asked.

"If you get us the meat and the sahlep,

I think we can help your mum," he said. "But it'll be risky."

Half an hour later Al was stuffing sahlep mixture into a large leg of pork. Then he tied a strong rope to the meat. Carrying the bundle, the boys climbed a steep hill to find Snotty, who was now fleeing along the cliff edge, the dragon not far behind her.

"OK," said Al. "I'm going to run between Snotty and the dragon, dragging the meat. The smell should be much stronger than Snotty's and hopefully the dragon will chase the new scent. That will give time for Snotty to escape. Then I'll drop the pork and run for my life."

"Wow," said Grenda, "that's a great idea."

"Wish me luck," said Al, as he bravely picked up the meat, wrapped the rope tightly around his hand and took off towards the pirate.

It didn't take him long to cut in behind Snotty, drop the meat to the ground and race into the dragon's path.

The creature quickly picked up the fresh scent and swerved towards Al. But the dragon was faster than he'd realised and gained in on him, jaws snapping.

Al ran blindly along the edge of the cliff for a few seconds, using all his strength to get ahead of the monster, until a rocky outcrop

blocked his way. Instinctively, he glanced down, wondering if he should jump, but to his horror he saw Greeny Joe circling in the ocean below. As Al looked behind him in desperation he realised the dragon was upon him.

Without thinking, as the dragon bolted towards him with its jaws open, Al tossed the leg of pork high into the air. The dragon sprang to grab the meat, its furious

momentum carrying it over the cliff, almost wrenching Al's arm from its socket in the process. Al had forgotten that one end of the rope was still wrapped around his hand.

He dug his feet into the earth to stop himself being dragged forward, but just before he reached the cliff's edge, the dragon's razor-sharp teeth bit through the leg bone and the pull on the rope slackened.

Al fell back on the ground, bruised and out of breath. The rope had cut him painfully. As he began loosening it from his damaged hand, he was surprised to find half a leg of pork still hanging from the other end.

Jack, Mahoot and Grenda were soon at his side. Realising the dragon had fallen into the ocean, they lay on their stomachs and looked over the cliff. The dark blue waters churned and frothed as Greeny Joe and the dragon tore at each other with fang and claw. Eventually, Greeny Joe seized the thrashing dragon by the neck, rolled over and dived. The ocean bloomed with blood and gore, and Greeny Joe surfaced again and again to feast on his kill.

Al was about to throw the mangled meat into the ocean when his eye caught something in the flesh that glinted darkly. While the others were still watching the terrible scene below, Al carefully removed the black diamond from the pork and slipped it into his pocket.

Grenda, who'd seen enough of the bloodshed in the ocean, turned and gave Al a beaming smile.

"Thank you," she said. "I know Mum isn't someone most people would help."

"No worries," said Al. A huge smile spread across his face as he realised just what he had accomplished.

"I won't forget this," said Grenda, "and somehow, some day, I'll make it up to you. I promise."

Meanwhile, Gunner and his pirates were back in the crypt, filling chests and casks with more treasure.

As the pirates worked, Gunner kept eyeing the golden sarcophagus. "Such a beautiful treasure," he told himself. "I can't just leave it here for Snotty to take after we leave. I'm gunner have to get it first." Spying a bolt of silken cloth, he tore at it, making crude gloves from the shreds. "If the mask's poisoned then these will protect me," he muttered, as he bent over the mummified sorcerer. He gripped the dazzling death mask with both hands and tried to prize it away from the body, but it remained stubbornly in place. Needing more leverage, he clambered onto the coffin, braced his feet and pulled harder. Still the golden mask refused to budge, so Gunner steeled his muscles and wrenched

upwards in one final show of might.
There came a snap from inside the coffin.
A strange blue light flared under his hands,
as if a fuse had been lit. An explosion
knocked him backwards and a fearful
splintering above Gunner's head shook
the ceiling.

Too late, Gunner realised the crypt
was a giant booby trap. "Run!" he
shrieked, as a piece of rock from the
ceiling plummeted with a crash onto the
sarcophagus. "Drop everything and run!"
he shouted again, struggling to his feet and
scrambling towards the crypt door.

As rocks hurtled around him and the
coffin was pummelled to pieces, Gunner
and his men bolted from the crypt. They
just managed to fling themselves out into
the courtyard as choking clouds of dust
erupted from within. Gunner lay coughing
for several minutes before he could breathe.

As the dust settled, the crew from *The Invincible* stared in horror at the buried tunnel and their lost treasure.

Ambush

Meanwhile, the most hated pirate in the Dragon Blood Islands, Blacktooth, was out on the high seas hunting for both treasure and revenge.

Shortly after Blacktooth's boat had been sunk in a battle between himself, Snotty Nell and Gunner, he had been rescued from the seas by a small trading boat.

Blacktooth, however, true to his formidable reputation, had turned on his rescuers, and hiJoeed the ship. Now he was back in action.

Blacktooth particularly wanted to avenge Captain Gunner because he'd seen the Dragon Blood Sabre on board *The Invincible*, hanging from a scabbard at a cabin boy's waist. Blacktooth knew all about Al and his friend Jack, and even more about the legendary sabre. The thought of the magical weapon made Blacktooth's blood fire with greed. Should he get his hands on it, he would be rich beyond his wildest dreams! "I'll have that ssabre for my own," he promised himself. "One day it will be mine!"

But after weeks of unsuccessful hunting for *The Invincible*, Blacktooth realised he had to reach his old adversary another way. "If I can't find Gunner," he reasoned, "I'll let him find me." He turned to his bosun, Pigface McNurt. "Gunner often goes to Ssabre Island," he said, "to vissit Mahoot'ss grandfather. Sso ssteer a coursse in that direction."

Once anchored there, Blacktooth led
a heavily armed gang of cut-throats to
Mahoot's grandfather's house. While the
old man worked in the garden, Blacktooth
grabbed him and pushed him into a chair,
tying him tightly. "We don't want you
warning anyone we're here," he growled,
checking the ropes one last time before
setting off with his crew to set an ambush.

Blacktooth made himself at home, set sentries to watch for a sail, and waited. Before long a breathless pirate arrived to tell them *The Invincible* had dropped anchor nearby.

Gunner was whistling happily as he marched through the jungle. He was looking forward to a good party on the beach and burying their small treasure.

Al, Jack and Mahoot were bringing up the rear, talking and laughing, looking forward to telling Mahoot's grandfather all about their adventures. In the bright sunshine, and feeling safe on Sabre Island, Al didn't notice the eyes on his ring glowing brightly.

As they rounded a corner, Blacktooth jumped out from the forest, waving his sword. "Drop what you're carrying, you lily-livered land-lubbers!" he demanded.

Gunner leapt into action, drawing his sword, but several brigands, who came from behind, swiftly disarmed him. Slicer and Mozzy joined the fray, wielding knives and cutlasses, but they too were overwhelmed.

Al looked around wildly for a way to escape, but Blacktooth's pirates had them surrounded. Making the most of the confusion, Al quickly took the black

diamond from his pocket and popped it into his mouth without anyone noticing.

Moments later Flash, Blacktooth's cabin boy, burst from the bushes smiling triumphantly. "My lucky day!" he jeered as he swaggered towards Al. "You are so going to pay for all the times you've annoyed me."

Al stared defiantly back at the bully and Jack spoke out in support of Al. "Still cutting up Blacktooth's food, you big waitress?"

Flash pulled his sword, whipping the blade through the air. "Not so brave now, are you?" Flash smirked, as Jack jumped back. "You're my prisoners and you'll do what I say. Empty your pockets, bilge rats!"

Not wanting to enrage Flash further, the boys pulled their pockets inside out.

Disappointed at not finding anything valuable, Flash shoved his face close to Al's. "You're a stupid snarfing seabass!" he spat.

Al couldn't say anything, so he looked past his tormenter as if he didn't exist.

Flash whipped his sword through the air again, bringing it up under Al's chin. "What are you?" he shouted, pressing the sharp point into his skin. "You're a snarfing seabass. Go on, say it, "I'm a stupid snarfing seabass"."

Al kept staring straight ahead, despite the

pain of the sword. He would have liked to do what Flash said, but he couldn't think how he could say snarfing seabass with a large diamond stuck in his mouth.

Infuriated by Al's defiance, the bully's face darkened. "You stinking, uppity, lice-infested lick-spittle," he growled, pushing Al backwards brutally.

As Al hit the ground hard he spontaneously swallowed the diamond. The gem caught in the back of his throat. He tried hard to swallow, but the diamond was stuck near his windpipe. Trying to conceal the fact he was choking, Al's face grew redder and redder and tears sprang to his eyes.

"Blubbering beetroot face," said Flash, enjoying Al's obvious discomfort. As Al lay suffocating, Flash spied his dragon-head ring and wrenched it from his hand. "This is mine now," he said, forcing it onto his finger.

Flash was interrupted as Blacktooth came

over and brought his fist down on Al's chest.
The impact dislodged the diamond and it slid
down to his stomach.

"Where'ss the ssabre?" Blacktooth
demanded. "Gunner ssays you don't have it."

"I don't," said Al, coughing and trying to
get his breath. "I lost it overboard."

"Liar! Gunner told me you hid it,"
Blacktooth snarled.

"I only said that so he wouldn't be angry
at me for being so stupid," Al lied, and his
face grew redder than ever.

"I hate liarss," said Blacktooth. "You had
the Dragon Blood Ssabre. I ssaw it with my
own eyess on Ruby Island. I don't believe
anyone could be ssuch an idiot ass to losse a
treasure like that."

"We were playing a silly game," Jack
chimed in. "And the next thing it slipped
out of Al's hand and, splash, we didn't have
it anymore."

"Two liarss," said Blacktooth.

"You haven't lost the sabre!" yelled Gunner, overhearing the conversation. "You couldn't be so stupid! I'm gunner kill you myself if you're telling the truth."

"Captain Gunner, I swear on pirate's oath," said Al. "The sabre's not on me, or the ship, or anywhere in the Dragon Blood Islands."

The truth in his voice was so real that Blacktooth paled. "It's losst!" he cried. "It wass found and then it wass losst by a sstupid boy." He pulled away from Al's chest. "You're going to be sso ssorry," he hissed. Blacktooth turned to Pigface. "Take Gunner'ss treassure back to our boat," he ordered. "The resst of you, tie thesse boyss up on the edge of the beach. I want them to

watch their friendss die as punishment for
their sstupidity."

Several hours later Blacktooth sailed away
from Sabre Island with Gunner's treasure,
leaving Al, Mahoot and Jack firmly tied to
the trees on the edge of the beach. In front
of the boys, buried deep in the sand, was
the crew of *The Invincible*. Their heads were
exposed to the sun, and they stared at the
boys with terror in their eyes, as the tide
turned and water lapped towards them.

"Help!" cried Gunner as a little white crab
emerged from the sand and scurried over his
head.

"Do something, please!" called Slicer.
"I can't stand it any longer."

The boys pulled frantically at their ropes.
Blood seeped from Al's wrists as he struggled,
but the ropes wouldn't budge.

"What can we do?" cried Jack, shaking

with the effort of trying to break free from his bonds.

"Grandfather! Help!" shouted Mahoot, hoping he would come to their rescue.

"He's not coming," said Jack, worried that Mahoot's grandfather had been murdered by Blacktooth.

"Mahoot!" he cried, his heart filling with hope at a sudden idea. "Can you call the elephants?"

"What can they do?" asked Mahoot.

"They could pull the men from the sand," said Al. "I know you can talk to them. Try to get them to understand we need help."

"It's worth a try," Mahoot agreed. He tipped his head back and made a loud trumpeting noise. Within seconds an answering call came from the jungle. Mahoot called again, and soon four elephants lumbered onto the beach and made their way to their friend.

The elephants seemed to listen with

interest to Mahoot's strange grunts and rumbling groans. After a few tense seconds they turned towards the beach.

"They haven't forgotten it was Gunner who saved their calves," said Mahoot. "They'll pull the men out."

To the boys' delight, the huge animals stopped before the pirates and, using their trunks, scooped the sand away from the men before wrapping their trunks around them and heaving them from the sand.

One by one they carried the pirates up the beach to safety, leaving them above the tide line.

Minutes later the freed crew had untied the boys.

The boys then raced to Mahoot's grandfather's house and released the old man from his ropes.

Waiting Game

The following day, Gunner and his men sank into despair. Grumbling and complaining about how unlucky they were, they went back to their boat and scrubbed the decks. Al and Jack couldn't stand all the complaining, so they went to Alleric Castle, leaving Mahoot some time alone with his grandfather.

As Al and Jack sat on the stairs in front of the castle, Snakeboot trotted out of the jungle and jumped into Al's lap.

"Can we go home, Snakeboot?" asked Al, stroking his pet. "We've had enough of the Dragon Blood Islands today, and we're missing the twenty-first century."

Snakeboot purred.

"It does seem ages since we were at home," Jack agreed.

In answer, Snakeboot jumped from Al's lap and ran into the castle. "I hope he's showing us a way back to Drake Drive," said Al, as the boys leapt to their feet and followed the cat.

The three raced up stairs and along corridors, before finally stopping outside a small room. Al stepped inside.

Immediately, a familiar tingling in his arms and legs told him he was leaving the Dragon Blood Islands for a journey though space and time.

Seconds later he found himself standing in his grandfather's magical sea trunk inside his attic in the twenty-first century.

Jack appeared beside him, shimmering and ghostly, until he slowly solidified. "We're back!" he cried happily.

Al looked around and waited for a few seconds. "Snakeboot hasn't come with us," he said. "He must have stayed behind."

"Perhaps he left us because we failed to get the diamond from the dragon and now the scabbard can never be repaired," said Jack sadly. "He probably feels there's no point coming with us anymore."

"We did get it, though," said Al with a smile.

"What?" cried Jack in surprise. "What do you mean?"

Seeing Jack's incredulous face, Al explained how he'd found the diamond.

"But where is it now?" Jack asked, amazed at the story. "It can't be on you, because Flash would have got it."

"I accidently swallowed it," Al admitted.

"We'll have to wait for it to come out the
other end. Then we can put it back on the
scabbard."

"Yuck!" said Jack, and he began to
laugh. "I think I'd rather stick my hand
in a dragon's mouth!"

Captain's Code

Can you decipher the following
message written in code?

6(L7, W2)   20(L18, W1)   23(L4, W3)
40(L5, W5)

Check out
www.dragonbloodpirates.co.uk
for the answer...if you dare!

(Clue: use this book to work out what it says.)

Arrr! Ahoy there, mateys!
Hoist the sails and drop the anchor: ye have some treasure to find!

One swashbucklin' reader will win an ipod Touch and ten runners up will win a Dragon Blood Pirates booty bag. For a chance to win, ye must dare to unearth the treasure!

Each of the six Dragon Blood Pirates: **The Legend of Dragon Island** books contain a clue. When you have solved the six clues, enter the answers online at www.dragonbloodpirates.co.uk

Or send your name, address and answers to:

Dragon Blood Pirates:
The Legend of Dragon Island
338 Euston Road, London NW1 3BH

Best o' luck, me hearties!

To find where the pirate treasure lies,
ye must find the answer to the clue that lies below:

This frightful Pirate drinks special tea,
It gets her into trouble that she did not foresee.

www.dragonbloodpirates.co.uk

Ahoy there shipmates!

To reel in amazin' pirate booty, steer smartly
towards www.dragonbloodpirates.co.uk

Ye'll find games, downloads, activities and
sneak previews of the latest swashbucklin'
Dragon Blood Pirates adventures.
Learn how to speak all pirate-like, how to find
out what type of pirate ye be, an' what pirate
games ye can play with yer mates! This treasure
trove is a sure feast fer yer deadlights!

Only the bravest an' heartiest amon' ye
can become a true scurvy dog, so don't
ye miss a thing and sign up to yer newsletter
at www.dragonbloodpirates.co.uk!

Don't ye miss book ten in the
Dragon Blood Pirates
series!

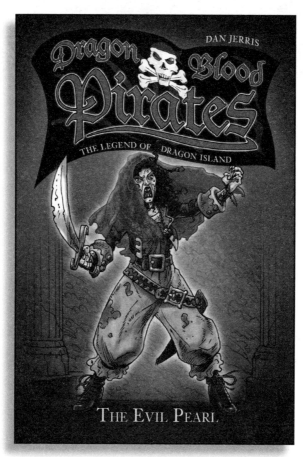

Turn the page and shiver yer timbers
with a slice of the next high-seas adventure...

The Magic Ring

"What do you mean my ring's magic?" asked Hally, inspecting a dragon-headed ring set with a pearl in its mouth.

"Your ring was made by the same sorcerer who made the Scabbard of Invincibility and the Dragon Blood Sabre," her brother, Al, told her.

"And we'd like you to lend it to us for a few hours," said Al's best friend, Jack. "We're not actually sure it's magic."

"Well, is it or not?" asked Hally. "I'm confused."

"We found out about your ring from a book in Alleric Castle," Al tried to explain. "My ring had magical powers, but that pirate kid, Flash, stole it. So come on, let's borrow yours. You're not using it."

"Let me see if I've got this right," said Hally. "You want to take my ring to the Dragon Blood Islands but leave me behind? I don't think that's very fair."

"But you don't like sailing," argued Jack.

Al winced at Jack's words. Hally didn't like being told what she didn't like.

"I didn't know my ring was magic," said Hally. "Besides, I haven't played princesses for ages. I might want to come with you."

"What if we're captured by Blacktooth or Snotty Nell?" Jack shuddered just to remind Hally how horrible they were.

"You're just a little girl who gets scared,"

said Al. He quickly regretted his words as
Hally stamped her foot and her eyes flared.

"I am not just a little girl," she said.
"I don't always get scared, and you're
not getting rid of me that easily!"

"We're not trying to get rid of you," said
Al. "All we want to do is see if your ring
can help us find another black diamond for
the Scabbard of Invincibility. We've got two
already, but we think Vicious Victor gave us

your ring on purpose, to help us in
our quest."

"In that case," argued Hally, "since that
ghostly old pirate gave the ring to me,
I would think he wanted me to use it,
which means I should come with you."

"Well, I suppose you can come then, if
you're brave enough," said Al, giving in.
"You've got ten minutes to get ready and if
you're not in the attic by then, we're going
without you."

When Al and Jack got to the attic they
changed into their pirate clothes, unlocked
the old sea trunk with an iron key and were
about to step inside when Hally appeared
at the door. She wore a long, old-fashioned
dress and the pearl ring was glowing on
her finger.

"Why aren't you wearing your scabbard
and sabre?" she asked her brother.

"Because the pirates want them," said Al. "I'm leaving them here in case we're chased for them."

"You're not scared, are you?" mocked Hally. "You're not just a little girl?"

"I'm not scared," Al snapped. "I'm just being sensible."

"Well, I'm brave," said Hally, "and you're not!"

"Fine, I'll wear them then," Al responded defiantly, pulling a dazzling silver scabbard with two enormous black diamonds from a cupboard, along with a golden sabre with a large ruby in the handle. He placed the sabre in the scabbard and strapped it to his waist.

"Well, Prince Alleric, you do look fine,"

said Hally in her princess voice. "Now I'm ready to go to the Dragon Blood Islands. Lead the way."

Al wished someone would pour cold water on his sister's silly ideas.

"Where are we headed this time?" asked Jack as Al stepped into the trunk.

Before Al could think of an answer he and his companions shimmered, became transparent and vanished from the twenty-first century and the suburban home at number five Drake Drive.

Watery Landing

Al found himself plummeting into the ocean. He kicked desperately for the surface and, seconds later, Jack popped up beside him, eyes round with shock.

Hally, too, struggled above water, gasping for air, and swam towards her brother. "Al!" she cried. "How come we're in the sea?"

"I don't know," replied Al, treading water to stay afloat, remembering his silly wish. "I just stepped into the trunk without thinking."

Jack looked around wildly. "We're way out in the ocean. There's not even an island nearby."

"And I can't swim very well," Hally whimpered. "What if we drown?"

"It's okay, we can hold on to the scabbard," said Al. "As long as we do that we can't die."

"But we can never let go of the black diamonds or we'll die instantly," said Jack. "The black diamonds make you deathless. Even if you died you'd be strangely alive..."

Hally began to sob. "I should've stayed home!"

"We should float on our backs and hold hands so we don't get separated," said Al, trying to calm his sister. "We've got to save our strength to stay alive."

The children floated for several minutes, but their heavy clothes began to drag them down. "I wish there was something to hold me up," Hally wailed, struggling against the folds of her dress.

Al lifted his head to search the ocean for something that might give them support or help, and his eyes caught a movement about a hundred metres away. A fin! His stomach lurched. He shut his eyes and tried not to panic. Somewhere he'd read that sharks were attracted to violent movements and sound. He didn't think he should make matters worse by telling the others they were about to be eaten alive.

He opened his eyes again, hoping the fin had gone away, but it was moving ever closer and, worse, several more were cutting the water further out. He shut his eyes again. Now there were at least six sharks. Black diamonds or not, they were doomed!

Something nudged his leg and a terrified shout escaped his lips. Hally and Jack looked around and, seeing the fins so close, also screamed in panic.

A dark shape moved right beside Al's head. There was a sudden whoosh of air and he was lifted from the ocean. After his initial horror, Al realised with a surge of relief that it was just a dolphin!

One by one the other friendly creatures swam up to the children.

"They're helping us!" cried Hally, as they were gently pushed along.

The dolphins took it in turns to lift the children and stop them sinking. Feeling more confident, Al reached out and held onto a dorsal fin. "Grab their fins," he told the others. "They might tow us."

To their delight, the children found themselves travelling through the ocean on the backs of a pod of dolphins, until they came across a dead tree bobbing in the waves. When the trio clambered onto the floating wood, their rescuers swam away.

"I wish I could thank them," said Hally, and in an instant the dolphins returned, nudging her with their noses.

"Thank you," said Hally, patting each dolphin's head. In turn, each creature squeaked, flipped its tail, did a wonderful somersault and was gone.

Alone again, at first the children felt quite safe, but as the day wore on, the log became unbearably uncomfortable and Hally started to grumble and complain. The bobbing swells took them nowhere and, by afternoon, the churning ocean and chilling breeze had finally exhausted her. She sat silently with the others, watching the horizon.

Just before dark a sail appeared, then a ship tacking in their direction.

"It's the *Nausi VIII*," said Al, recognising the wallowing boat as it came closer.

"Not Snotty's ship!" groaned Jack. "She hates us!"

"And she'll probably steal the sabre and scabbard," said Al, regretting he'd ever brought them back.

"And my ring," said Hally. "I'd better hide it in my dress."

"I can't hide the sabre," said Al, "but maybe she'll be nicer than usual because we saved her life last time we were here."

And so, despite their fear of Snotty Nell, exhausted by the ocean, the children waved and called out to attract attention.

Mermaid Island

The dripping children were soon standing before Snotty Nell. "What are you lot doing out here?" she asked, her one good eye never leaving Al's sabre and scabbard. "Gunner's ship hasn't sunk by any miracle?"

"No," answered Jack. "He's still sailing The Invincible."

"We weren't with Gunner," explained Al. "We were playing and just got caught by the ocean."

"Dolphins rescued us," said Hally.

"And pigs might fly, young Hally," snorted Snotty.

"Princess Halimeda to you," Hally corrected, annoyed at being called a liar.

Snotty stiffened at her words, but turned on Al. "You're wearing something that little boys don't deserve to have." She wiped her nose on her sleeve and held out her hand for the sabre and scabbard. "I heard they'd been found and I didn't believe it. Give them to me and I won't feed you to the fishes."

"What are you going to do with them?" asked Al as he reluctantly unbuckled the scabbard and sabre and held them out to Snotty.

"Learn how to use the sabre's magic," said Snotty, pulling the weapon from its sheath and waving it through the air, "and tomorrow I'll dump you on Mermaid Island when we stop for water."

"Are there mermaids there?" asked Hally, excited.

"Of course there are, dear," said Snotty, with a smirk that twisted her scarred face. "And they're expecting a princess for morning tea."

"What about a town?" enquired Al, wondering how he was going to get his scabbard and sabre back.

"Deserted," said Snotty. "And now that I've saved your life, I don't owe you a thing. We're even. So don't you go bringing up how you stopped that dragon from eating me."

"I wasn't going to," said Al, "but I was hoping for a bit better treatment than being abandoned on an island."

"Well, as you so kindly gave me this wonderful sabre, I'll give you some provisions," said Snotty. "Now it's off to the brig with you." As they moved from earshot, she turned to her first mate, Vampire Zu.

"Take them below and keep watch on them. They're trouble. I don't trust them to be left on their own for a second. And don't tell my daughter they're on board. They have a habit of turning her soft."

The following morning Vampire Zu and a small crew of pirates collected the children from the brig, lowered them into a longboat and rowed them ashore.

Once on the beach the pirates clambered

out. "While we're collecting water you can unload your supplies," said Vampire Zu, pointing to a tarpaulin at the stern of the longboat. He glanced up at the sky and signalled to his brigands to unload the water barrels. "We'd better hurry, mateys. There's a storm coming. Snotty's on a bad anchor."

As the pirates left, Al moved to the back of the longboat and pulled back the tarpaulin. He jumped when a voice said, "I bet you didn't expect to see me!"